MEG'S EGGS

for Katie

MEG'S EGGS

by Helen Nicoll
and Jan Pieńkowski

PUFFIN BOOKS

It was suppertime, so Meg
got out her cauldron

She
put
in

lizards, newts, 2 green frogs

They could not break the eggs

Meg's egg was hatching

Meg took Diplodocus to

the pond

Diplodocus was very happy

Mog was sleeping by his egg

BUMP   THUMP

ZZZ
ZZZ
ZZZ

when he heard a noise

Mog
took
Stegosaurus
into
the
garden

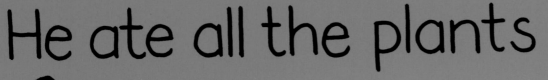

Owl
was
watching
the
last
egg

TAP

TAP

Out
jumped
Tyrannosaurus,
the
most
ferocious
of
all
the
dinosaurs

They
were
very
frightened

Tyrannosaurus wanted to eat them all.

Meg flew home and tried
to make a good spell

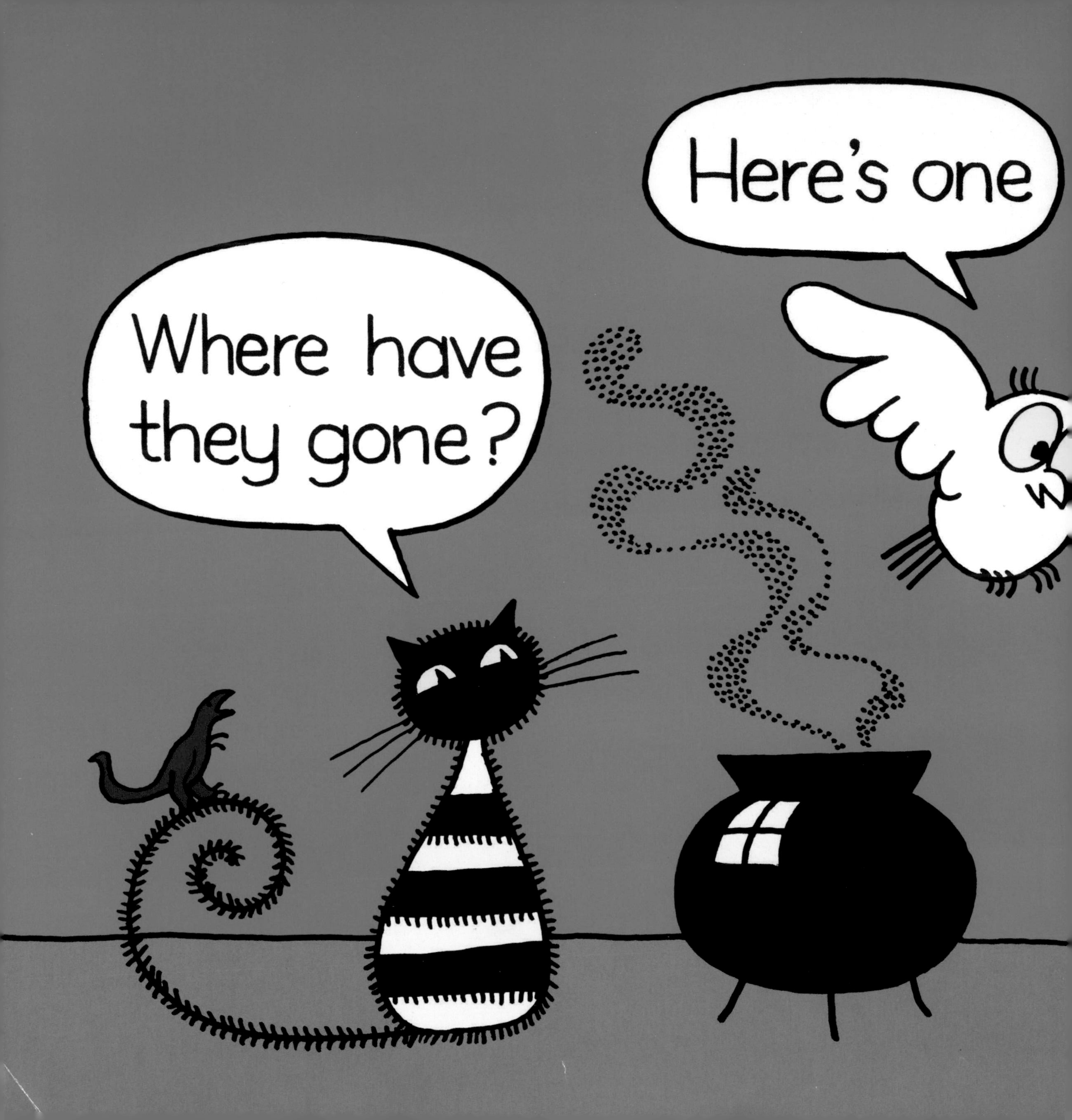
Here's one
Where have they gone?

Goodbye!